MW00941891

Piggie Sue
Finds A Friend

Melisa Brown

MCP BOOKS

MCP Books
2301 Lucien Way #415
Maitland, FL 32751
407.339.4217
www.millcitypress.net

Printed in the United States of America

Hard Cover ISBN-13: 978-1-6322-1769-1
Ebook ISBN-13: 978-1-6322-1770-7

Dedication

For my friends and family who support me unconditionally and to my fur family for loving me the same way. These individuals (fur and human) make my world a better place.

A special and heartfelt "thank you" to Kris Muller, who kindly and generously illustrated this book as a graduation present when I "finally" finished my master's degree.

It's a beautiful day!
I'm tired of being at home
wondering what to do.
I am just so bored
and want someone to play with...
Maybe I'll go to the zoo.

I'll talk to everyone
and I'll find a friend...
maybe I'll even find two.
A beautiful day
to find a friend.
I'm off to go to the zoo.

I wish she wouldn't say that,
said Sweet Dodo the cat.
What's wrong with me? Boo hoo!
I'm a friend and a cat.
How about that?
And I am not at the zoo!

When Piggie Sue got to the zoo,
she met a monkey or two.
She went straight in
and called yoo hoo.
Will you be my friend,
my monkey friend 'til the end?
Hey there, hello, yoo hoo.

But, the monkey just squealed
and swung back and forth
Ee ee ahh ahh oo oo.
Piggie Sue looked confused,
didn't know what to do.
Could she not
find a friend at the zoo?

She sighed and decided
to visit the lion.
She felt so sad already...
she was almost cryin'.
Will you be my friend?
She looked up and said.
Rooooaaaaar! said the lion
as he tossed back his head.

Piggie Sue sat down
and just stared, amazed.
But, the lion didn't move.
He kept his fierce gaze.

He Roared once again
and she decided to go.
Well, that's one more down.
No friends, none to show.

She walked to the place
where the elephants stood.
Will you be my friend? she asked.
I'll be good!

The elephant stomped
and blew his trunk like a trumpet,
a loud blast.
Piggie Sue knew
she had to get out of there fast.

Confused and so sad,
Piggie Sue stood looking up.
From her eyes, tears fell,
what a sad little pup.

Guess I'll go home.

I didn't find any friends here.

Piggie Sue pouted and shuffled,

her crying so clear.

She got home

and she went to the sofa to sit.

Just where Sweet Dodo

had been waiting a bit.

I'll be your friend,
Sweet Dodo the cat
said with pride.
Come in and sit down,
let's chat side by side.

And, just then it occurred
to little Piggie Sue you see.
Home is where the heart is
and best friends too, indeed.